Dear Parents:

Congratulations! Your child is taking the first steps on an exciting journey. The destination? Independent reading!

STEP INTO READING® will help your child get there. The program offers five steps to reading success. Each step includes fun stories and colorful art or photographs. In addition to original fiction and books with favorite characters, there are Step into Reading Non-Fiction Readers, Phonics Readers and Boxed Sets, Sticker Readers, and Comic Readers—a complete literacy program with something to interest every child.

Learning to Read, Step by Step!

Ready to Read   Preschool–Kindergarten
• big type and easy words • rhyme and rhythm • picture clues
For children who know the alphabet and are eager to begin reading.

Reading with Help   Preschool–Grade 1
• basic vocabulary • short sentences • simple stories
For children who recognize familiar words and sound out new words with help.

Reading on Your Own   Grades 1–3
• engaging characters • easy-to-follow plots • popular topics
For children who are ready to read on their own.

Reading Paragraphs   Grades 2–3
• challenging vocabulary • short paragraphs • exciting stories
For newly independent readers who read simple sentences with confidence.

Ready for Chapters   Grades 2–4
• chapters • longer paragraphs • full-color art
For children who want to take the plunge into chapter books but still like colorful pictures.

STEP INTO READING® is designed to give every child a successful reading experience. The grade levels are only guides; children will progress through the steps at their own speed, developing confidence in their reading.

Remember, a lifetime love of reading starts with a single step!

Belle's
STORY
COLLECTION

DISNEY PRINCESS
Belle's
STORY COLLECTION

Step 1 and 2 Books

A Collection of Six Early Readers

Random House 🏠 New York

Contents

Happy Birthday, Princess! 9

Princess Hearts 31

Princesses and Puppies 61

Beauty and the Beast 83

A Cake to Bake 105

The Perfect Dress 127

DISNEY PRINCESS

Happy Birthday, Princess!

by Jennifer Liberts

illustrated by Elisa Marrucchi

Random House 🏠 New York

Belle's birthday party
is so much fun!

Belle shares cake
with everyone.

Gifts for Tiana.

Lights that glow.

Cinderella's gifts have
lots of bows.

A wish come true!

Golden lights.

18

Birthday candles
shining bright!

Balloons

for Snow White.

Friends who care.

Jasmine has lots
of goodies to share!

Play a game.

Have some fun!

Cupcakes
for Ariel!
Yum, yum, yum!

Happy birthday, Princess!

DISNEY
PRINCESS
Princess Hearts

by Jennifer Liberts
illustrated by Francesco Legramandi

Random House 🏠 New York

Valentine's Day
at the castle
is fun!

33

Cinderella gives hugs to everyone.

Rapunzel's gift
is tied in a bow.

A Valentine heart
makes the sky glow.

Red roses for Aurora
are so sweet!

A Valentine kiss

is always a treat.

Belle's love stories
are red, pink,
and white.

Valentine cupcakes
make a yummy sight!

Seven sweet
valentines
stand in line.

Snow White asks
her friends,
"Will you be mine?"

Jasmine has
Valentine candies
to share.

54

Ariel's gift
looks great
in her hair.

A Valentine parade
feels just right.

Tiana and her prince
dance all night.

Happy Valentine's Day!

DISNEY PRINCESS
Princesses and Puppies

by Jennifer Liberts

illustrated by Francesco Legramandi

Random House 🏠 New York

The Prince gives
Cinderella a puppy!

Cinderella's puppy
gives her kisses.

Who is hiding
in the flowers?

Rapunzel finds
a fluffy white puppy!

Rapunzel finds
the puppy's family.

Belle gets
to choose a puppy.

Belle picks

a wiggly puppy!

Merida sees a puppy.

He rolls in the mud.

Merida gives
the puppy a bath.
Splash!

A puppy wants
to play with Tiana.

The puppy naps
on Tiana's lap.

A puppy does a trick
for Jasmine!

Princesses love puppies!

STEP INTO READING®

DISNEY PRINCESS
Beauty and the Beast

by Melissa Lagonegro

illustrated by
the Disney Storybook Art Team

Random House 🏠 New York

Belle is kind
and smart.
She loves
to read.

Gaston wants
to marry Belle.
She does not
like him.

Belle's father, Maurice,
is an inventor.

He goes on a trip.

Maurice gets lost
in the forest.
Wolves surround him!
He finds a castle.
He goes inside.

Maurice meets
magical objects.
Lumiere is a candlestick.
Cogsworth is a clock.

The castle belongs
to the Beast.
He locks Maurice
in a cell.

Belle finds Maurice.
She asks the Beast
to free her father.

Belle meets

the magical objects

in the castle.

Lumiere sings.

Belle explores
the castle.
She finds a magic rose.

The Beast finds Belle.

He grabs the rose.

Belle is scared!

Belle leaves the castle.

Wolves surround her.

She is in danger!

The Beast arrives.

He fights the wolves.

He saves Belle!

Belle returns

to the castle.

She and the Beast

become good friends.

They spend time outdoors.

Belle teaches the Beast
to dance.

They are happy.

Belle sees her father
in a magic mirror.
He looks sick.

Belle leaves
to help him.
The Beast is sad
when Belle leaves.

Gaston wants
to find the Beast.
He goes to the castle.
He attacks the Beast!

The Beast is hurt.

Belle is very sad.

"I love you,"

says Belle.

The Beast

is really a prince!

Belle's love changes him

into a human.

They live happily

ever after.

DISNEY
PRINCESS

A Cake to Bake

by Apple Jordan

illustrated by Fabio Laguna & Andrea Cagol

Random House 🏠 New York

Princess Tiana loves
to cook.
But she loves
to bake even more!
She bakes brownies
and pies.

Merida is baking cookies.
Who will help her
gather eggs?

"Not me!" say her
brothers.
They are too busy
playing.

The cookies are done!
Who will help
eat them?

"Me! Me! Me!"
say the brothers.

There is a pie contest
at the fair.
Rapunzel is going to
enter her best pie!

She picks apples.

She makes a tasty crust.

There are so many pies
at the fair.

They all taste yummy!

Rapunzel's pie
is the best.
She wins a blue ribbon!

It is Eric's
birthday.
Ariel wants to
bake him a cake.

She has never
baked before.
The chef is too busy
to help.

Sebastian will help.

Scuttle will help, too.

Sebastian cracks the eggs.

Scuttle pours the milk.

Ariel mixes.

Ariel bakes!

Ariel decorates the cake.

What a mess!

Yum!

The cake tastes great.

Eric knows it was

made with love.

121

The Beast is sad.
Belle wants
to cheer him up.
She will make him
a special dessert!

Belle looks
in her cookbook.
Brownies would
be perfect!

Belle melts chocolate
and butter.
She mixes in
flour, sugar,
and eggs.

Belle bakes the brownies
in the oven.

The Beast is surprised!
He is happy to have
a sweet friend
like Belle.

The
Perfect Dress

by Melissa Lagonegro
illustrated by Elisa Marrucchi

Random House 🏠 New York

Dust and dirt
make a mess!

Cinderella needs
a brand-new dress.

Clean and bright.
Oh, what fun!

This blue dress is
the perfect one.

Jasmine must choose
a skirt or a gown.

Her friend Rajah
looks on with a frown.

Jasmine and Aladdin
enjoy a starry night!

Her green outfit
is truly just right.

Belle is excited about the fancy feast!

She gets dressed for
her date with the Beast.

Belle and the Beast
share a night of romance.

Her yellow gown is
perfect for this dance.

Everyone sings in
the wedding parade!

King Triton sends off
his little mermaid!

Ariel's wedding dress
fits just right.

Prince Eric thinks she looks lovely in white!

Sleeping Beauty has
such a busy day!

144

The fairies can help.

They are on their way!

Music and menus.

There is much to do.

Should Aurora's dress be pink or dark blue?

The Prince arrives with
his horse by his side.

Snow White must dress
for their royal ride.

It's chilly and windy.

It feels like a storm.

A blue and red cape will
keep Snow White warm.

Slip on the shoes.

Fluff up the dress.

Put on the jewelry.

Look your best.

Which one do you think

is the perfect dress?